My Furry Foster Family

Toby the Dog

written by Debbi Michiko Florence

illustrated by Melanie Demmer

raintree

a Capstone company — publishers for children

Thank you to Jocelyn, at Save One Soul Animal Rescue, for her help with my research — DMF

Raintree is an imprint of Capstone Global Library Limited, a company incorporated in England and Wales having its registered office at 264 Banbury Road, Oxford, OX2 7DY — Registered company number: 6695582

www.raintree.co.uk
myorders@raintree.co.uk

Text © Capstone Global Library Limited 2020
The moral rights of the proprietor have been asserted.

Designed by Lori Bye
Original illustrations © C
Originated by Capstone (

978 1 4747 8505 1

British Library Cataloguing in Publication Data
A full catalogue record for this book is available from the British Library.

Acknowledgements
We would like to thank the following for permission to reproduce photographs: Mari Bolte, 66, 69; Melanie Demmer, 71; Roy Thomas, 70

Every effort has been made to contact copyright holders of material reproduced in this book. Any omissions will be rectified in subsequent printings if notice is given to the publisher.

Printed and bound in India

Contents

Dad
(Tim Takano)

Mum
(Cindy Takano)

Me
(Kaita Takano)

Eraser

Ollie

Joss Lawrence,
Happy Tails
Rescue

Hannah Miller,
my best friend

CHAPTER 1

A special phone call

I held a dog treat in my hand.
"Ollie, sit!" I said.

My happy dog wagged his tail and
sat down.

"Good boy!" I said. I threw the
treat in the air. Ollie caught it in his
mouth. He crunched and crunched,
then he sniffed the floor for crumbs.
He didn't want to miss one.

"I think you've got them all, Ollie!"
I said, giggling.

"Kaita! I'm home!" a voice called.
It was my mum.

Ollie and I ran to the kitchen. The
tags on his collar jingled like little bells.

Mum had a pile of books on the
table. She works at a bookshop. I love
it because she gets me books about
animals. When I grow up, I want to
be a vet. I'm going to be the best
animal doctor ever!

"Are these books for me?" I asked.

"Yes," she said. "There's a book
about cats, a book about birds, a
book about dogs and a book just
about dachshunds, like our Ollie."
She slid the books in front of me.

I gave her a big smile. "Oh, thank you, Mum!"

Yip! Yip! Yip! Ollie barked and ran to the back door.

"That must be Dad!" I said, running after Ollie.

Yip! Yip! Yip!

Dad walked in, bent down, and patted Ollie's head. He got hugs from Mum and me.

"Coming home to my family is my favourite thing," Dad said. "I have some good news!"

"What is it?" I asked.

Dad smiled, but he didn't say anything. He took off his jacket. He hung it on the hook. He put his bag on the floor. He took off his shoes.

"Dad!" I said. "Come on. What is it?"

"Yes, stop teasing us," Mum said with a smile.

"OK, sit down at the table, and I'll tell you," he said.

We all sat down. Ollie curled up

under my chair.

Dad grinned. "I got a phone call from Happy Tails Rescue," he said.

I peeked under my chair. "That's where we got Ollie," I said.

We had adopted Ollie from Happy Tails Rescue last year. The poor little dog had been found in a car park with no collar and no home. Happy Tails took him in. They rescue animals and help them find forever homes. I was so happy we became Ollie's forever home.

"What did Happy Tails Rescue say?" Mum asked.

I wriggled in my chair.

"They have a dog who needs a foster family," Dad said.

"He needs love and a place to stay until he finds a forever home. And *we're* going to foster him!"

"Hooray!" I said.

"When?" Mum asked.

The doorbell rang. Ollie barked. *Yip! Yip! Yip!*

"Right now!" Dad said, jumping out of his chair.

Mum and I followed him to the front door. Mum scooped up Ollie in her arms.

It was Joss, the amazing woman from Happy Tails Rescue. "Hello, Takano family!" she said. "Thank you for agreeing to foster."

Ollie wagged his tail. I could tell he remembered Joss.

"Hello, Ollie!" Joss said, patting his head.

"Where is the dog?" I asked.

"Toby is in my van," Joss said.

"Will Toby like Ollie?" I asked.

"Toby is friendly to other dogs," Joss said as we walked to her van. "He is an older dog. He is a very sweet Labrador mix."

"What happened to his family?" I asked.

"Toby's family had to move far away. Sadly they couldn't take Toby with them," Joss said. "We will find him a wonderful new home and family."

When we got to the van, Joss opened the door and grabbed the lead. A black dog jumped out. He was bigger than Ollie. He stood closely against Joss' legs, like he was trying to hide.

"He is beautiful," I said.

Toby looked at me and blinked.

His tongue rolled out. His thick tail thumped against Joss.

"Look at that. I think he likes you, Kaita," Joss said.

I liked Toby, too!

CHAPTER 2

Hello, Toby!

Before Joss left she gave us a bag of Toby's toys. She gave us a crate, too. We put the crate in my parents' bedroom. Toby would sleep there. Ollie already slept with me in my room every night.

After dinner I worked on a puzzle with my parents. I like puzzles. They are fun to put together. Ollie curled up on my lap. Toby sat by the door.

"He seems sad," I said. "Perhaps he

wants to go home."

"This *is* his home now," Dad said. "It will take time for him to feel safe with us. He doesn't know us yet."

I dug into Toby's bag of toys and found a cuddly lamb. I threw it. It landed at his feet with a *plop*.

Toby sniffed the toy a bit but didn't move.

I got a tennis ball. I waved it in front of his face and rolled it past him. "Get the ball, Toby!" I said.

Toby watched the ball but didn't move.

Ollie did, though. He shot after the ball like a rocket. *Yip! Yip! Yip!*

Toby's ears went up. He wagged his tail and barked. *Woof! Woof!*

Ollie ran past him, and Toby followed just behind him. Just like that, the two dogs became friends.

***

The next day Ollie and Toby played tag. Ollie chased Toby from the living room to the kitchen, up the hallway and into my room. Toby chased Ollie out of my room, down the hallway, into the kitchen and to the living room.

Back and forth the dogs ran. They barked non-stop.

Dad got a bit cross. He was trying to talk on the phone for work.

"Come on, you two!" I said. "Let's play quietly in my room."

Ollie, Toby and I went to my room and sat on the floor. I pulled a bright-yellow rubber duck from Toby's bag of toys. Toby wriggled and whined.

"Do you want your duck?" I asked him.

Toby wagged his tail and licked my hand. I gave him the toy. He squeaked it a couple of times.

Playing tag had made the dogs tired. I lifted Ollie onto my bed. He curled up. Toby wanted to get on my bed, too, but I said no. Joss had told us to keep Toby off the furniture. His forever family might have a "no furniture" rule.

I got Toby's dog bed from his crate and put it on the floor.

"You can have a sleep over here, Toby," I said.

Toby sniffed his bed, snorting from end to end. When he had sniffed it all, he stepped onto the bed. He turned in a circle three times, flopped down and curled up tight. With a sigh he fell asleep.

"Good dog," I said.

Ollie watched me tiptoe to the door. I put my finger to my lips. "Shh!" I whispered. He stood and pawed at the air. He wanted to be picked up. I walked back to my bed and got him, then closed the door behind us.

While Toby slept I sat at the kitchen table with my sketchbook. It already had lots of Ollie drawings in it: Ollie in his alligator costume, Ollie chasing a ball, Ollie lying on his back with a big, full tummy…

Now I started drawing Toby. I wanted a way to remember him when he had found a forever home. I drew three pictures: one of him sitting, one of him with his rubber duck and one of him sleeping on his bed.

Yip! Yip! Yip! Ollie barked and ran to the back door.

"Mum's home!" I said.

Mum walked into the kitchen with her book bag. "Hello, Ollie!" she said. "Hi, Kaita! How is Toby?"

"Great!" I said. "He and Ollie have been playing tag all morning. Toby is having a sleep. He's in my room."

"Perfect. Let's take them for a good, long walk," Mum said.

I ran to get Toby, but when I opened my bedroom door – oh no! It looked like a blizzard had blown through my room!

Ripped paper covered everything like snowflakes. My rubbish bin was upside down. My desk chair was on its back. Toby was sitting in the middle of it all, his dog bed shredded to bits.

"Toby!" I shouted.

Ollie came running and stopped in the doorway. *Yip! Yip! Yip!*

I don't always have the neatest bedroom. Mum usually has to tell me to clean it. But this was a *disaster!*

Ollie looked at the mess Toby had made, then he sneezed.

Toby dipped his head. He tucked back his ears. He looked very sorry.

"Oh dear," Mum said when she saw my room. "Toby has made a bit of trouble, hasn't he?"

"Yes, he has," I said.

Ollie sneezed again and backed into the hallway.

I went over to Toby. I held his head in my hands. "Did you think we forgot about you in here?" I asked. "I'm so sorry. You're OK, Toby. Don't worry."

"Kaita, I'll take the dogs for a walk,"

Mum said. "You start cleaning your room. If you're still working on it when we get back, I'll help you finish."

I nodded. "Thanks, Mum."

"Ollie, time for a walk! You too, Toby!" Mum called, heading back to the kitchen. Ollie followed Mum, and Toby followed Ollie.

Mum and Dad had said that it would take time to learn how to foster pets. I learnt a good lesson that day: Never leave a foster dog alone in your room!

CHAPTER 3

Toby finds trouble

I wasn't the only one learning how to foster a pet. Mum and Dad were learning, too. Every day brought new lessons.

"Oh, Toby," Mum said, looking sadly at her ripped book bag. "You've found trouble."

"Oh, Toby," Dad said, looking at a chewed shoe. "You've found trouble."

"Oh, Toby *and Ollie*," I said, looking at a torn, empty box of dog treats. "You've found trouble." I gave both dogs' tummies a quick rub. "Well, at least you two are happy."

Dad, Mum and I quickly learnt our lessons. When we couldn't watch Toby, we put him in his crate. We made sure there was nothing he could rip or chew on the floor. Unlike short little Ollie, Toby could reach the worktop when he stood on his hind legs. So we cleared everything off it!

Our daily routine went like this: In the morning, before Dad took me to school, I fed Ollie and Toby. After school Mum and I took the dogs for a walk. During homework time Ollie slept on one side of me. Toby slept on the other. After dinner we played. At bedtime, when Dad read a story to me, Ollie and Toby listened, too.

The five of us were a happy, furry foster family.

***

A couple of weeks later, Mum and I came home to a big surprise.

Yip! Yip! Yip! Ollie greeted us at the door like he always did. But then –

Woof! Woof!

"Toby! How did you get out of your

crate?" I asked.

"Maybe I forgot to close the gate," Mum said.

Woof! Woof! Toby rose on his hind legs and licked my face.

I laughed and gently pushed him away. After that, my hand felt sticky. Why? Before I could work it out, Ollie ran into the other room. He usually followed me when I got home. Something wasn't right.

Toby wagged his tail. I saw a yogurt lid stuck to his back. The fur on his head looked matted and oily. Someone had found trouble!

"Mum?" I said, looking around, my eyes wide.

"Oh my goodness!" Mum cried.

"What is all of this?"

The bin had been tipped over. Dirty wrappers, broken eggshells, banana peels and other rubbish covered the kitchen floor.

Toby nudged my legs. Crisp crumbs dusted his nose.

"Eww! You stink!" I cried.

Toby's tongue hung out, as though he was smiling and pleased with himself. He ran to the middle of the floor and rolled around in the rubbish, back and forth. The eggshells crunched. He slid on the banana peels. He waved all four paws in the air. He was a very happy dog!

"Oh, Toby," Mum said. "You've found trouble! You need a bath."

I hurried to the bathroom and filled the bath with warm water. When Toby heard the water running, he ran into my room. He tried to hide under the bed. He did not want a bath!

Ollie poked his nose into my room. He smelt Toby, backed away and ran down the hallway. I didn't blame him. Toby was stinking up my room quickly.

"Toby, it's OK. We just want to clean you up," I said. "Baths are *fun*." I talked in a calm voice while Mum hooked his lead to his collar.

We walked Toby to the bathroom, and he sat down in the doorway.

That was it. He wouldn't go any further. Mum pulled. I pushed. The dog would not move.

"I don't get it. I thought Toby would like water because he's part Labrador retriever," I said.

"Every dog is different," Mum said.

That's when I had an idea. I ran to Toby's crate and got his rubber duck. Holding the toy over his head, I said, "Toby, get your duck!" I threw the toy into the bath. *Splash!*

Toby's ears perked up. He leaped. *SPLASH!* Toby was in the bath!

Mum and I quickly soaped him up. He sat still, with his toy in his mouth.

We scrubbed. We rubbed. We rinsed. Soon Toby was clean again.

He jumped out of the bath. *Shake! Shake! Shake!* He shook the water from his fur. Now Mum and I were all wet! We started laughing.

"You are a good dog, Toby," I said, hugging him.

CHAPTER 4

Old friends, new friends

Ollie, Toby and I had great fun together. We loved to go on walks and play fetch. The three of us made a good team.

I started to wonder if my family could be Toby's forever home.

One day my best friend, Hannah, came over. She liked Ollie a lot, but she was nervous about meeting Toby.

"Don't worry. He is such a terrific dog," I said to her.

Hannah and I went to my room. *Yip! Yip! Yip!* Ollie loved Hannah. He wriggled and squirmed like a puppy in her lap.

I ran to my parents' room and got Toby from his crate. He barked and licked my face. *Woof! Woof!* Before I could stop him, he ran down the hallway towards my room.

"Toby, wait for me!" I laughed.

When Toby got to my room, he stopped in the doorway. He saw Hannah sitting on my bed. He did not go in. I walked past him and sat next to Hannah and Ollie.

Toby stood and looked at us for a long time. He wagged his tail but stayed in the hallway.

"It's OK, Toby," I said. "This is Hannah. She's my best friend."

Toby sat down.

"Look. Ollie loves Hannah," I said. Ollie wagged his tail and licked Hannah's face.

Toby slowly stepped into my room. He crept to my side and stuck close to my leg, away from Hannah. He kept watching her.

"He can be shy with new people," I said. "It takes a little bit of time for him to feel safe." I remembered when Toby first met my family.

"Toby, I want to be your friend," Hannah said. "Do you want to be mine?" She held out her hand, palm up. She stayed very still.

Toby carefully leant across me. He sniffed her hand.

Hannah smiled. Toby thumped his tail.

"Good boy," she said.

Woof! Woof!

Toby licked Hannah's hand. She giggled. "Toby, you *are* a terrific dog," she said.

"I told you!" I said.

I was so pleased that all four of us were friends now! We grabbed some toys and went out into the garden to play.

"Kaita, you really like Toby, don't you?" Hannah asked.

"I do!" I said. "He's the perfect fit for my family!"

Hannah smiled, but she looked a bit sad, too. "It's a shame he can't stay here forever. It's going to be hard to say goodbye."

I didn't want to think about that.

∗∗∗

Dad made my favourite dinner that night: hamburgers with fried eggs. Just as we were sitting down to the table, Mum said, "Guess what?"

"What?" I asked.

"Joss called me today. She might have a family for Toby," she said with a smile.

"That's great!" Dad said.

I looked down at the floor. On one side of my chair was Ollie. On the other side was Toby. What would it be like when Toby wasn't here anymore? I felt a tug in my heart – and a lump in my throat.

"So what happens next?" I asked. I leant down and patted Toby's head. I rubbed his ears.

"Joss will make sure the family is good for Toby," Mum said. "After that the family will call me or your dad. They'll ask us questions about Toby, and we'll tell them everything about him. If they think he sounds like the right dog for them, they will come to our house to meet him."

"Make sure you tell them he needs a crate," I said. "Tell them he eats things that are not food, like rubbish and blankets. Remember what he did to your book bag? And Dad's shoe? Remember the mess in my room?"

"Yes, we will tell them the truth

about Toby," Dad said. "We want Toby to find his forever home."

"Make sure you tell them he doesn't like baths. Tell them he is shy with new people," I said.

Mum put down her hamburger and looked at me. "We will also make sure we tell them all the *terrific* things about him, too. He loves other dogs. He knows how to sit, come, stay and lie down. He plays fetch. And he is very loving."

"Are you sad about Toby leaving, Kaita?" Dad asked.

I didn't feel like eating anymore, even if it was my favourite dinner. I looked down at my plate and nodded.

"Kaita, we talked about this, remember?" Mum said.

"I know, I know," I said. "Toby's just so…"

"By fostering we are helping a lot of animals, instead of just one or two that we would be able to adopt," Mum continued.

Dad reached over and rubbed my shoulder. "I know it's hard, Kaita," he said. "You've done a great job with Toby! He's had a safe, loving home away from home with us. We've taught him good manners. We also learnt what makes him special, so we can help him find a good match with another family."

Mum's eyes got a little wet. She smiled and said, "No matter what happens, Toby will always have a place in your heart. He'll have one in your dad's heart and my heart, too."

I knew all of this. Of course I wanted to help animals, but I had fallen in love with Toby. How could I say goodbye?

CHAPTER 5

A terrific dog

The family that Joss told us about was not the right fit for Toby. They called and talked to Dad. The family loved to go fishing, and they wanted a dog to take to the lake. Dad told them he wasn't sure Toby would like the lake. Toby hated baths. To Toby a lake would seem like one big bath!

A day later a man called and

talked to Mum. He wanted a quiet house dog, one he could leave in his house while he went to work. Mum told him that Toby sometimes chewed things like blankets or rugs when he was alone. He wouldn't be a good fit for the man.

Another week went by.

"Joss says that older dogs are harder to find homes for. Many people want puppies," Mum said.

"Toby is house trained. That makes things *easier* for a family," I said.

Dad nodded. "True," he said. "Does this mean you aren't sad anymore about finding a home for Toby?"

I was still a little bit sad about Toby

leaving, but I was sadder that nobody wanted to adopt him. He was a good dog. He deserved a forever family.

Finally, four days later, Mum had good news. "Mr and Mrs Garcia and their son, Ben, are coming to the house on Saturday to meet Toby," she said.

"Did you tell them everything?" I asked. "Did you tell them that Toby is terrific, but that sometimes he finds trouble, too?"

"I did. They thought his antics were funny," Mum said.

I crossed my fingers. I loved having Toby here with us. But I wanted him to find his own home.

On Saturday morning I tidied my room. I gathered all of Toby's toys and put them in his toy bag. Dad put Toby's bed next to the bag by the front door. We didn't know if this family would be a good fit. We hoped they would be.

The doorbell rang.

Yip! Yip! Yip! Woof! Woof!

I put Ollie in my room. I didn't want him to distract the Garcia family from Toby.

Mr Garcia was tall. He smiled a lot. Mrs Garcia wore jeans and a T-shirt with a picture of a dog on it. Ben was older than me, almost a teenager. The minute he saw Toby, he kneeled down.

Toby hid behind my mum.

I looked at Ben. I was worried that he would be upset, but he just smiled. I kneeled down too. "It's OK, Toby. These people want to meet you," I said.

Toby peeked around my mum's legs and looked at me. Then, wagging his tail, he walked over to Ben and licked his cheek! Ben laughed.

"He is beautiful," Mr Garcia said.

Toby went to Mrs Garcia and sat down in front of her. "What a good boy!" she said, patting his head.

"He is terrific," Ben said, turning to me. "Your dad said he sometimes gets into trouble. I do, too!"

"It looks like you and Toby will become best friends," I said.

"I hope so," Ben said.

"I think Toby will be perfect for our family," Mrs Garcia said. "Can we take him home?"

I handed Toby's lead to Ben. Mr and Mrs Garcia gathered Toby's things. I let Ollie out of my room so he could say goodbye.

Just before it was time for him to leave, I hugged Toby, tight. "Have a wonderful life with your new family," I whispered in his ear. He licked me one last time. Mum, Dad, Ollie and I watched the Garcia family and Toby drive away. Toby looked very happy.

"How are you feeling, Kaita? OK?"

Mum asked.

"I think so," I said. "I'm a bit sad, but mainly happy."

Yip! Yip! Yip! Ollie crawled onto my lap and nuzzled my ear. I was happy he had found his forever home with us. I was happy Toby had found his forever home with Ben, too.

***

Life at my house went back to its normal routine. Every morning I fed Ollie his breakfast. Every afternoon after school, Mum and I took him for a walk. Every evening he sat next to my chair as I did my homework. Every night he curled up on my bed to sleep.

Two weeks later Dad showed me an email from Mrs Garcia. She said that they all loved Toby. Ben and Toby went to the park every day. Attached to the email was a picture of Toby with his rubber duck in his mouth. He was sitting on Ben's bed. I don't think they had a rule about no dogs on the furniture!

Later that night, while I was doing a puzzle, Ollie ran to the back door. *Yip! Yip! Yip!* Mum was home from the bookshop.

"Kaita! Guess what?" Mum said excitedly.

"What?" I asked.

"We have another foster pet coming!" she said.

"Really? Hooray!" I cried.

I jumped, then started dancing with Ollie. All kinds of thoughts spun in my head. What kind of animal would we get? Another dog? A cat? Something more unusual, like a snake or a rabbit? I couldn't wait to find out. I was ready to help another animal find its forever home!

Think about it!

1. How does Toby tell Kaita that the rubber duck is his favourite toy?
2. How are Ollie and Toby different from each other? Give three examples.
3. Do you think Toby is a terrific dog? Why or why not?

Draw it! Write it!

1. Kaita likes to draw. What is your favourite animal? Draw a picture of it.
2. Kaita worries that Toby might not find his forever home. Write a short newspaper advert that tells readers why they should adopt Toby.

Glossary

adopt look after as one's own

antics playful or funny acts

crate cage

dachshund dog with a long body and short legs

distract draw attention away from something

foster give care and a safe home for a short time

Labrador retriever strong, medium-sized dog

routine set of tasks done in a specific order

Fact or fiction:
Who is Kaita?

Kaita Takano is the main character of the My Furry Foster Family series.

Did you know that there is a real-life Kaita? Just like the Kaita in the series, she has a miniature dachshund called Ollie and she fosters animals with her family.

The Kaita in this book is fictional - that means "made up" or "imaginary". A writer of fiction makes things up to tell a story.

Non-fiction is based on fact (true, real things). There is nothing made up in non-fiction. Story Kaita likes to read lots of non-fiction books about animals so that she can learn more about them.

Eraser

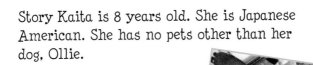

Story Kaita is 8 years old. She is Japanese American. She has no pets other than her dog, Ollie.

Story Kaita enjoys putting together jigsaw puzzles and drawing animals.

Real Kaita is 10 years old. She is half-Korean American, half-European American.

Real Kaita enjoys knitting, sewing and playing computer games with Ollie.

The Kaitas are similar in some ways, too. They both love to draw and read.

Story Kaita reads non-fiction books about animals. Real Kaita enjoys graphic novels best, but she also likes to read non-fiction. Neither Kaita has brothers or sisters. They both live with their mum and dad.

CAT CARE

BIRD FACTS

DOG · BREEDS

And the biggest thing the two Kaitas share?

Nothing makes them happier than helping pets find their forever homes!

Wait! The two Kaitas do share one more, very important thing: They think you're fantastic for reading this story!

About the author

Debbi Michiko Florence writes books for children in her writing studio, The Word Nest. She is an animal lover with a degree in zoology and has worked at a pet shop, the Humane Society, a raptor rehabilitation centre and a zoo. She is the author of two chapter book series: Jasmine Toguchi and Dorothy & Toto. Debbi lives in Connecticut, USA, with her husband, a rescue dog, a rabbit and two ducks.

About the illustrator

Melanie Demmer is an illustrator and designer based in Los Angeles, USA. She has created artwork for various clothing, animation and publishing projects. When she isn't making art, Melanie enjoys writing, spending time in the great outdoors, iced tea, scary films and taking naps with her cat, Pepper.

Go on all four fun, furry foster adventures!

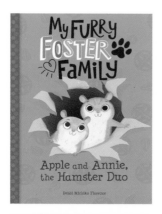

Apple and Annie, the Hamster Duo

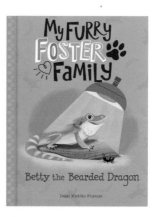

Betty the Bearded Dragon

Buttons the Kitten

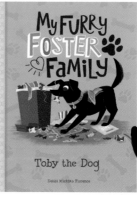

Toby the Dog

Only from Raintree!